The Lamp,
the Ice, and
the Boat Called *Fish*

Based on a True Story

Jacqueline Briggs Martin
pictures by **Beth Krommes**

HOUGHTON MIFFLIN COMPANY
BOSTON

To my mother, who also knows about sewing. – J.B.M.

To Dave, Olivia, and Marguerite, my own little family. – B.K.

Author's Note: The story of the *Karluk* (kar-LUKE) and its survivors is true. And it is true that the Iñupiaq family brought a seal oil lamp with them. There may also have been an Iñupiaq grandmother who gave the gift of a song with the lamp. Songs are important to the Iñupiat and they are given as gifts.

I would like to thank Debby Edwardson, Emily Ipalook Wilson (Makpii's daughter), and their Iñupiaq friends and relatives in Barrow, Alaska, for their help and advice on Iñupiaq names, vocabulary, and other details of this story. I have tried to be as careful with the story as Qiruk was in sewing boots. What errors remain are mine and not theirs. And I would like to thank my editor, Ann Rider, a good companion and trail-finder on any journey to new territory.

Some of the books read in researching this story:
Bartlett, Robert. *Northward Ho! The Last Voyage of the* Karluk. Boston: Small & Maynard, 1916.
Brower, Charles D. *Fifty Years Below Zero*. New York: Dodd, Mead, 1965.
Chance, Norman A. *The Iñupiat and Arctic Alaska*. New York: Holt, Rinehart & Winston, 1990.
McKinlay, William Laird. Karluk: *The Great Untold Story of Arctic Exploration*. New York: St. Martin's Press, 1976.
Wilder, Edna. *Once Upon an Eskimo Time*. Anchorage: Alaska Northwest Publishing, 1990.
——. *Secrets of Eskimo Skin Sewing*. Anchorage: Alaska Northwest Publishing, 1976.

Illustrator's Note: Thanks to Pamela Ross for all of her help and time and for sharing her Alaskan experiences.

Text copyright © 2001 by Jacqueline Briggs Martin
Illustrations and illustrator's note copyright © 2001 by Beth Krommes

www.houghtonmifflinbooks.com

Library of Congress Cataloging-in-Publication Data

Martin, Jacqueline Briggs.
The lamp, the ice, and the boat called *Fish* / by Jacqueline Briggs Martin ; illustrated by Beth Krommes.   p.   cm.
Summary: Tells the dramatic story of the Canadian Arctic Expedition that set off in 1913 to explore the high north.
ISBN 0-618-00341-X (hardcover) ISBN 0-618-54895-5 (paperback)
1. Iñupiat – Juvenile literature. [1. Canadian Arctic Expedition (1913–1918) – Juvenile literature. 2. *Karluk* (Ship) – Juvenile literature.
3. Arctic regions – Discovery and exploration – Juvenile literature.] I. Krommes, Beth, ill. II. Title.
E99.E7M295 2000 919.804–dc21 99-35303 CIP

ISBN-13: 978-0618-00341-9 (hardcover)
ISBN-13: 978-0618-54895-8 (paperback)

Printed in Singapore
TWP 10 9 8 7 6 5 4 3 2 1

The Seal Oil Lamp

In the high North, in the summer,
when day never ends
an Iñupiaq (in-YOU-pea-ack) grandmother walked out from her house—
one of the last of the old sod houses.

She walked under the eye of the sun and the flying raven.
And she listened to the song of the land, the wide sky,
the sound of the wind, the ptarmigan.
She knew she would walk many hours searching for moss—
moss to be wicks for the seal oil lamp—
the lamp carved from stone by her husband
long ago when they had both been young.

It was his first gift to her
and was as much a part of the old woman as her voice
or the ugruk (OOG-rook) sewing case she always carried.
Now she would be the one to give the lamp away.
It would go where she could not go.

The old woman gathered many pieces of moss,
then sat in front of her house.
Her granddaughter sat beside her
and they worked together shaping the moss into ropelike wicks for the lamp.
The grandmother sang of the place,
the wide sky, the sound of the wind, the ptarmigan.

She told the girl,
"You are going on a boat for a long time.
Take this lamp and the song. Take part of your home."
Then the girl went with her mother, father, little sister,
and her father's friend. They climbed into an umiaq (OO-me-ack)
and rowed out to the white men's boat, the boat called Fish.

1. The Boat Called *Fish*

Pack ice: The sea ice that covers northern oceans for much of the year.

The boat was built in the 1880s to carry salmon
and was named *Karluk*, Aleutian for "fish."
After a while it carried crews
to hunt bowhead whales.
Then the whaling stopped, and the *Karluk* had no work—
until the summer of 1913,
when it sailed north from British Columbia
toward the Arctic Circle.

There were no fishing crews and no whalers on board,
but scientists of the Canadian Arctic Expedition,
traveling up the coast of Alaska to study the plants and people in the high north.
The leader of the group was an explorer named Stefansson.
He wanted to find new islands in the icy ocean.
There were also a cook, a captain, a crew, one black cat, and forty sled dogs.

When the boat reached Point Barrow
Stefansson invited an Iñupiaq family to join the expedition.
Stefansson knew the group would need fur clothes
and boots of caribou and sealskin to survive the Arctic cold.
They would need fresh meat from seals and *ugruk* – bearded seal.
Qiruk (KEE-rook), the mother, could look at a man,
cut a fur skin with her round-bladed *ulu* (OO-loo), and sew a pair of pants
that would fit him exactly.
She could make boots that would keep his feet from freezing.
Kurraluk (KOO-ra-look), the father,
and his friend Kataktovik (KUT-uk-tow-vik) were good hunters.
They had the patience to wait by seal holes for hours.
Qiruk and Kurraluk brought their two daughters.
Pagŋasuk (PAG-na-sook) was eight years old and little Makpii (MUK-bee) was two.

The crew built a place on the deck for the family to live.
Inside their small room they had a seal oil lamp
that gave warmth and light.
Perhaps the two girls had a ball,
made of sealskin and filled with caribou hair, to toss and catch.
The crew never heard them cry.
They played while the forty dogs howled and fought
and the black cat ran in the galley.

Winter came early in 1913,
and soon the captain
was steering the ship between huge chunks of ice—
some as big as houses.

In mid-August the boat was stopped
by a large sheet of ice, up to a foot thick
and dotted with water holes.
As the weather grew colder the water
thickened with gray needles of new ice.

While Paŋnasuk and Makpii tossed their sealskin ball,
while the carpenter taught tricks to the black cat,
while the sled dogs scrapped,
and while they all slept,
the ice around the boat froze solid.

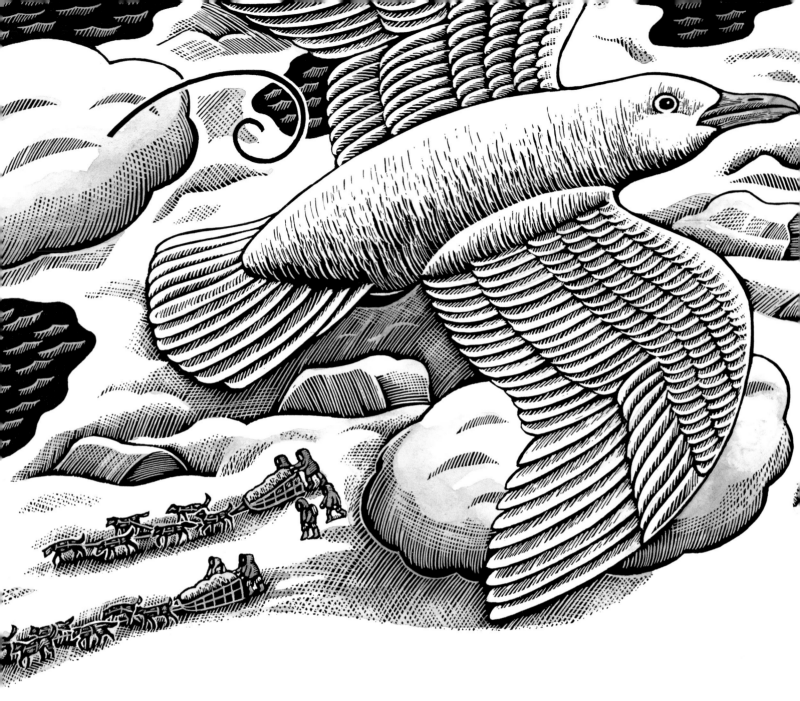

Then the boat and the ice were one,
and the boat could go only where the ice went.
That was when the leader, Stefansson, and five others left the boat
with sleds and dogs to hunt caribou.
They were on land when a storm blew the ice-locked boat out to sea.
Stefansson sent a report to the government in Ottawa
that the *Karluk* would probably be sunk by ice
but he was sure its passengers would survive.
Then Stefansson was off to look for new land.

II. Locked in the Ice

Floe: A piece of sea ice. Floes can vary in size and grow up to many square miles. In one winter an ice floe might grow to a thickness of one yard. An ice floe will continue to grow each winter. If it is not crushed by a larger piece of ice, it can reach a thickness of thirty feet or more.

That was when the boat's captain, Robert Bartlett, became the leader.
That was when Qiruk sewed every day.
No one could tell what would happen.
Would the boat sink? Would they have enough food?
Would they be able to stay warm in the cold, dark winter?
As long as the ice was solid the boat was safe.
If the ice should crack,
then wind or water would be strong enough
to push a piece of ice through its wooden sides
and the boat would sink.

I do not think Pagnasuk and Makpii worried about the boat.
They knew about cold. They were born into cold.
And they trusted their father and mother to keep them safe.
I think they sat by the lamp and played with their ball.
And perhaps Qiruk had made them dolls from sealskin.
She knew the secrets of sewing
and might have made tiny fur parkas for their dolls.

While they played, Qiruk sewed boots
for all the people on the boat.
For the leg of each boot she used the skin from caribou legs
that she had scraped until it was soft and strong.
For the sole she used the skin of the ugruk.
She shaped it by chewing it,
then pinching it with her thumb and fingers.
When the shape of the sole was just right
she set it to dry.
It took Qiruk a whole day to sew one sole to one boot top.
But when she was done, the boots were strong and watertight.
Without those boots, feet would freeze and people would die.
Qiruk used her ulu to cut fur skins for pants
and parkas for the crew and the scientists,
and she showed them how to sew their own clothes.
They called her Auntie.

Every day Kurraluk and Kataktovik went out on the ice
to look for seals.
They brought back enough fresh meat
for the twenty-five people on the *Karluk,* the twenty-eight dogs, and the cat.

For three months the boat continued to drift in its icy trap—
wherever the wind and water took it.
The crew and the scientists used boxes and barrels
to build the walls of a house on a large ice floe not far from the ship.
That ice was thirty feet thick and half as big as a football field—
"able to stand a good deal of knocking," the captain wrote later.

In December, while the ice shifted, groaned, and scraped around him,
Kurraluk worked in the Arctic twilight
and built a house of snow next to the box house.
Mr. Hadley, the ship's carpenter, made three long sledges, or sleds.
They all knew that if the ship did sink,
they would have to haul their clothes and food supplies to land.

They kept themselves busy and even had holidays.
When Christmas came,
the captain, the Iñupiat, the scientists, and the crew
feasted on oysters and bear steak, cake and biscuits.
The captain gave Auntie a comb, a looking glass, and a new dress.
He gave Makpii and Paŋasuk new dresses, too.
And he gave Kurraluk and Kataktovik new hunting knives.
They ran races and had a tug of war, and everyone was jolly.
No one talked about when the boat might sink.

On New Year's Day they went out on the ice to play soccer.
Qiruk was goaltender.
The air was so cold the captain could not blow the whistle.

Nine days later, at the end of the day,
when Pagŋasuk and her sister may have been sitting by the seal oil lamp,
listening to their father tell stories of a ten-legged polar bear,
they heard a loud, splitting sound.
A large, sharp point of ice was breaking through the side of their boat!
"All hands abandon ship!" the captain called.
He sent Qiruk and the two girls
to the box house to start a fire in the stove
so all would have a warm shelter.
The others carried supplies off the ship and onto the ice floe.
The carpenter took the black cat to the box house in a basket.
They could not see where they were going in the dark night and blowing snow.
The ship's doctor fell into the sea and had to be pulled to safety.

After everyone else had left the *Karluk*,
Captain Bartlett sat in the galley, next to the stove,
and played records on the ship's record player.
He called it his duty to stay with the ship until it went down.
When each record was finished, he threw it in the stove's fire.
The captain played music all night long and all the next morning.
Slowly, slowly, water filled the ship.
By afternoon he knew it was time to leave.
He put on the last record, Chopin's "Funeral March,"
and stepped onto the ice.
He took off his hat and said good-bye to the boat.

Everyone stood outside to watch the *Karluk*
as it disappeared underwater.
By the next morning the ice was solid.
The *Karluk* was locked under the sea.
The thirteen crew members, the captain, the six scientists,
the Iñupiaq family, their friend Kataktovik,
the dogs, and the cat
were left on an island of blue ice in the cold, dark Arctic.

III. The Island of Ice

The sounds of ice: Cracks that form in the ice and widen into leads, or lanes of open water, often quickly freeze over with new ice. As new ice is pushed against the old ice, the weaker piece breaks. This constant pushing, breaking, and piling of ice results in groaning, scraping, thrumming sounds. Sometimes when the ice cracks, it sounds like a gunshot.

They called their place Shipwreck Camp.
The box house on the floe was warm and snug.
It had only one room, smaller than a schoolroom.
At one end of that room was the kitchen with a cookstove.
Another stove sat in the center of the room.
On three sides, built against the wall,
were bed platforms made of wood taken from the boat.
Makpii, Paŋŋasuk, and their parents had their own sleeping room,
with its stove and bed platforms,
made of snow, connected to the box house.
And they all ate together.

Once they were all settled in at Shipwreck Camp,
Qiruk and the men began sewing again.
Without the right clothes,
people could not make the long journey
over the sea ice to Wrangel Island.
They sewed the fur clothes by hand
and had two sewing machines for the other clothes.
They used lanterns and lamps for light.
There was still no sun,
only twilight in the middle of the day.

But they must have had the seal oil lamp.
The burning seal blubber would have made their little room
on the ice smell like their home near Point Barrow.
While they listened to the eerie music of the ice,
perhaps Paŋnasuk watched the flame and sang her own song
of the wide sky, the sound of the wind, and the ptarmigan
to little Makpii and the sealskin dolls.

One day in January
Kurraluk, Kataktovik, and five of the crew left to find Wrangel Island.
The Iñupiaq men knew how to travel over sea ice with dogs and sleds.
The captain wanted four crew members to stay on Wrangel Island
and begin setting up a new camp.
The other three could help on the journey and then return
to Shipwreck Camp.

While they were gone the sun came back to the sky,
ending seventy-one days of twilight and dark.
Everyone in the box house celebrated with oyster soup.
After supper they gathered around the stove.
Someone made music with a comb and the others sang.
The captain liked to dance. I can see him dancing with the carpenter.
Qiruk sang hymns the missionaries had taught her.
Pagnasuk sang "Twinkle, Twinkle Little Star."

One day, when the captain thought the three travelers would surely return,
he ordered the crew to build a fire with thirteen sacks of coal,
a wooden boat, and ten tins of gasoline.
He wanted to be sure Kurraluk and the others could see the fire
and find the small camp among the huge fields of ice.
But no one came.

There might have been trouble.
Travel over sea ice is dangerous.
Sometimes the new ice is soft and travelers fall through
into the deep cold water.
Sometimes it cracks and breaks away and a person is trapped
on a piece of ice floating out to sea.
And there is always the worry of frozen toes, frozen feet, frozen fingers.

Every day Qiruk, Makpii, and Paŋasuk
would climb a hill of ice
and watch for men with dogs and sleds.
Maybe Paŋasuk practiced tossing and catching sticks
because it reminded her of her father.
Maybe she looked into the seal oil lamp and heard
her grandmother singing the song of home.
And she did not feel so lonely.

Then one day, on the hill of ice, they heard sled dogs barking.
Even though they could not see him,
they knew their father was coming home.

The travelers had not gone all the way to Wrangel Island
because they had come to a lead, a space of open water, too wide to cross.
The four crew members said they would wait until the lead froze over
and then walk over the ice to the island.

As the days went by
the captain began to worry about the men
still on their way to Wrangel Island.
He decided it was time to leave Shipwreck Camp.
Qiruk repaired snowshoes.
Kurraluk and Kataktovik put long handles on their snow knives
so they could build each iglu more quickly
when they had to stop at night.
They knew it would take many days to walk almost one hundred miles
from their camp to Wrangel Island.
The day before they left, everyone took a bath
and put on clean underwear.
There would be no changing of clothes once they started.

They left in the early morning, when it was still dark.
The black cat was tucked into a sack
the men had made for her and rode on top of one sled.
Kurraluk, Qiruk, Makpii, Pagnasuk, and the cook
took another sled, loaded with supplies.
Qiruk carried Makpii on her back.
Pagnasuk helped her father and five dogs pull the sled.
They went out into the dark over the sea ice toward land.

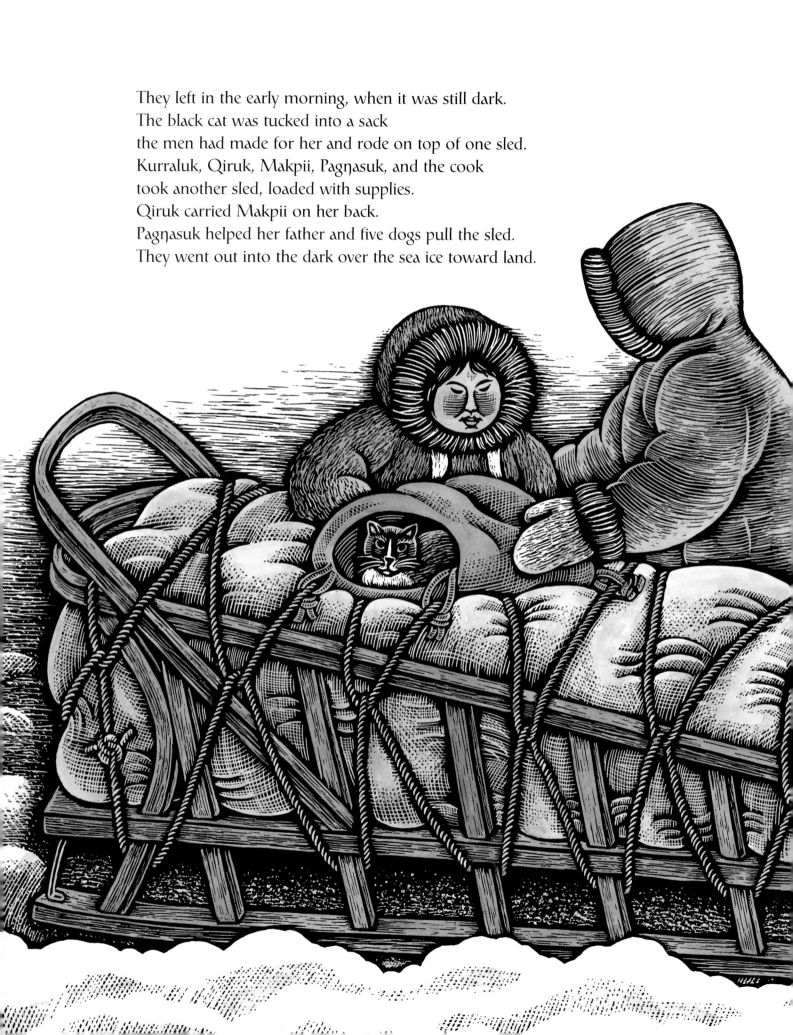

IV. Across Sea Ice

*Hummock: A ridge or pile of crushed sea ice. Hummocks are formed
when two areas of ice are pushed against each other by wind or current.
They can be more than one hundred feet tall and can extend for miles.*

They were not walking over the smooth ice
that freezes over skating rinks and inland lakes
but over rough ice piled and tumbled by wind and water.
Pagnasuk's sled had to stop many times
so Kurraluk and the cook could chop the ice
with heavy picks and axes and make a trail.

And it was cold, so cold their hands would freeze in a minute
if they forgot and took off their mittens.

Paŋasuk wore long fur pants
that started at her toes and went up to her waist,
a fur shirt with the fur next to her skin, a fur parka with the fur facing out,
boots lined with dry grass, and fur mittens.
She had to wear goggles, too. Otherwise, the sun and snow
would cause snow blindness. Some wore goggles of amber glass.
Paŋasuk probably wore Iñupiaq goggles of wood with thin slits in the eyepieces.
Makpii didn't have to wear as many clothes
because she rode inside her mother's parka.

The travelers walked, then chopped, walked, then chopped,
and were able to travel about thirty miles in the first two days.
In the afternoons they stopped in time to build three iglut for the night.

Each iglu needed a floor—a place where the ice was firm
and would not crack and slip them into the ocean.
Then with long snow knives they cut blocks of snow.
They used big blocks for the bottom of the snow house.
Snow houses are often round, but on this trip they built square houses.
And instead of making a round snow roof, they used their tents.
Inside the snow house, along the wall, they built a platform of snow for a bed.
They put their fur sleeping robes on the bed and slept with their clothes on.
If the ice cracked, they had to be able to move quickly.
After the iglu was built,
they made a half-circle door to crawl through.
When everyone was inside, they closed the door
with a block of snow.

In Paġnasuk's little house,
Qiruk would light the lamp, light the stove, and make tea.
They all ate a supper of dried meat and fat, called pemmican, biscuits, and tea.
After supper they climbed onto their snow beds and fell asleep.

Though they were careful to look for strong ice,
they did not always find it.
One night a thunderous crack split the ice
under the family's iglu.
Their floor was suddenly gone,
leaving a lane of dark, cold water.
Little Makpii nearly fell in,
but Qiruk snatched her up
and they rushed outside.
The captain gave his iglu to the family for the rest of the night.
Maybe Qiruk cradled the children to sleep with a song.
But she surely stayed awake until morning listening to the ice crack and groan.

Before they could reach the island
the travelers had to cross huge hummocks of jumbled ice,
ridges that went straight up, sometimes as much as one hundred feet.
The captain said they were like a small mountain range.
He had never seen worse ice.

They could not walk through the ridges.
The dogs could not pull the sledges through these hills.
They had to use picks and axes to make every step of the trail.
Some of the men wanted to quit.
But Captain Bartlett pushed them on.
He knew they would die
if they did not get to the island.
Once they worked for five days chopping and digging
to make a three-mile path over the mountains of ice.
Finally, after seventeen days of travel
Kurraluk shouted, *"Nuna, nuna"* (land, land),
and they stepped off the ice onto solid ground and Wrangel Island.

V. The Hungry Summer

Melting ice: Long days of sunshine cause the ice to break up in the late spring and early summer. The leads of open water become too wide to cross on foot. The ice bridge is gone.

The hilly island was about seventy-five miles long
and thirty miles wide.
When the people from the *Karluk* arrived,
the island was covered with snow.
There were no trees
but many pieces of driftwood on the beach.
They looked for the four crew members
but never found them.

Kurraluk built three iglut at a place called Icy Spit.
Qiruk worked hard by the fire drying out boots and stockings.
She mended tears and
tried to make boots and clothes strong again.

After six days, when the captain's clothes were dry
and his sled dogs were rested,
he and Kataktovik left to walk two hundred miles across the ice to Siberia.
They had to walk fast before the ice bridge across the sea melted.
If the captain could get to Siberia,
he could telegraph a message for a rescue boat.
He said he would come back in the middle of July.
He left on March 18.

After the captain and Kataktovik left,
three of the *Karluk* people moved sixty miles away to Rodgers Harbor
so everyone would not be hunting in the same place.

They were all trying to solve one big problem—
finding enough food for themselves and the dogs.
(The cat did not work and lived well on scraps.)
There were no caribou, no reindeer, and few bears.
They had enough pemmican to last until summer.
But when they ate only pemmican they got very sick.
Two men at Rodgers Harbor died from eating pemmican.
They did not learn until later that the pemmican
had too much dried meat and not enough fat,
and so was poison to their bodies.

They tried many ways of finding food.
Kurraluk hunted nearly every day.
In April he brought in two large and two small bears
to share with the eleven others at Icy Spit.
In May, when they moved into tents because
their snow homes were melting, Kurraluk found seal.
At every meal Qiruk saved back a part of the food
and put it in her tin box for the hungry time
when Kurraluk would not find bird or seal or bear.

One day Qiruk began to be sick from the pemmican.
Her feet and legs swelled and she had no strength.
Pagŋasuk took little Makpii and walked along the island, looking for food.
They wanted to help their mother, but they found nothing.
Then Kurraluk brought in two seals.
They had fresh meat. They made soup.
Qiruk began to get strong again.

In June the Iñupiaq family,
the carpenter, and a Scotsman called Wee Mac
moved to a place on the island called Cape Waring,
where there were more birds.
They slept in the same tent and ate together at the same fire.
Four of the crew members at Icy Spit moved, too, and shared a tent nearby.
Two went to Rodgers Harbor.

Near the time of the midnight sun
Pagŋasuk and Makpii found a dead owl,
and Qiruk made them a stew.

Every day they worked to find food
for themselves and the dogs.
The carpenter and Wee Mac made a chair
with rope and pieces of driftwood.
Then the carpenter lowered the wobbly chair and Wee Mac
over the edge of the cliff. The little scotsman sat in his chair
and collected birds' eggs from cliffside nests.

Wee Mac wrote later, "July was a hungry month.
We ate seal tails and flippers and
sometimes chewed on sealskin."
Even when there were only scraps
the others always made sure Pagnasuk and Makpii ate first.

In July Kurraluk decided to build a boat
so he could hunt on the water.
He used a hatchet to carve the frame from two large logs.
Then he and Wee Mac used skinning knives to whittle it to the right size.
Kurraluk carved a paddle and scraped sealskin for the outside.
Qiruk sewed the skins together over the frame with caribou sinew.
The day after the qayaq (KYE-ack) was done,
Kurraluk went out in it and brought back a walrus.

At the end of July
Kurraluk shot three ugruk.
They feasted on fresh meat and hung some to dry.
In two months it would be winter again.
The captain still had not come.
Perhaps he had died on his journey. Perhaps he would never come.
If they had to spend winter on the island,
they would need much food.

For four weeks in August the hunters had no luck.
They ate the dried meat they were saving for winter.
Some days they ate only soup made from month-old scraps or walrus skin.
Paɣŋasuk may have remembered the Iñupiaq story of a magic lamp
that could find its own seals for fat to burn and meat to eat
and wished her lamp had such power.

But Kurraluk did not wait for a magic lamp.
He was a hunter and would not quit.
When he had no more bullets for his gun
he practiced throwing sticks.
He brought thirty crowbills down with his stick.
He caught birds with a net.

Pagŋasuk and her mother
used sinew and a bent pin to catch a fish called tomcod.
Makpii and Pagŋasuk gathered the tough woody roots of an island plant.
Qiruk cooked them every night.
The roots made Wee Mac sick, and he couldn't eat them.

In early September the snows began again.
Their fur clothes were worn and thin.
They did not have enough food for winter.
They hoped for the captain
but they looked for food every day.

Qiruk and the two girls caught more tomcod.
One day Pagŋasuk trapped a gull.
Her mother made a thin stew.
They all worked hard
but could not forget the coming cold
and days of certain hunger.
They did not know if they would see another spring.
But little Makpii always said, "We'll be all right."

One morning in September
Qiruk, Makpii, and Paǧnasuk fished for tomcod
and caught enough for breakfast.
While they cooked, Kurraluk went
to look for wood to make a spear.
"Umiaqpak kanna!" they heard him say.
"Big boat down that way!"

VI. Umiaqpak Kanna

(OO-mee-ack-pack kun-na)

Landfast ice: An area of ice connected to coastal land and extending outward, sometimes for many miles.

They looked out to sea
and saw the first ship they had seen
since the *Karluk* sank eight months ago.

But would the crew on the ship
see the small figures and ragged camp on the island?
Would they even think to look for people on the island?
The carpenter fired his gun.
Kurraluk went running out over the land-fast ice.
The *Karluk* survivors could not know
Captain Bartlett had asked these walrus hunters to detour
past Wrangel Island and offer emergency help.
The ship lowered its sails,
and several of its crew went out onto the ice.

Wee Mac, the carpenter,
Qiruk, Kurraluk, Paŋasuk, Makpii, and the others
were too hungry to leave the tomcod on the beach.
They ate the fish and drank tea before they packed their few belongings.
I think they brought the seal oil lamp and the dolls.
They left their worn tents on the island, walked across the ice,
and climbed onto the ship called the *King and Winge*.
Once on board they all took baths and ate bread and butter.

Captain Bartlett had traveled hundreds of miles.
And he had spent much of his summer in Nome
looking for a ship to go to Wrangel Island.
In July he found the fifty-year-old *Bear* but then lost more weeks
in failed attempts to get through the Arctic pack ice.
In September, the *Bear* refueled and headed out for one last try before winter.
Finally, the day after the rescue, the old ship caught up to the *King and Winge*.
Bartlett greeted the twelve survivors and helped them move over to the *Bear*,
where there was a doctor to tend the sick and frostbitten.
He watched Paŋasuk and Makpii carry the black cat onto the ship.

After five days they arrived in Nome.
Qiruk, Kurraluk, Paŋasuk, and Makpii left the ship
to start their long journey
up the coast of Alaska to Point Barrow and home.

And when they arrived,
perhaps they lit the seal oil lamp inside the sod house –
one of the last of the old sod houses –
and told their grandmother their story
of the boat that sank, the long walk over the ice, the hungry summer.
Then they sang the song of home,
the wide sky, the sound of the wind, the ptarmigan.
And the black cat sat and listened.

The Passengers of the *Karluk*

I have told of some of those on board the *Karluk* when it first went north into the Arctic Ocean. But the story is not complete without a list of all those who were on the ship called *Fish* when it became trapped in the ice.

Vilhjalmur Stefansson, expedition leader, left the *Karluk* in September to hunt caribou. He stayed in the high north for five years.

Diamond Jenness, anthropologist, left the boat with Stefansson and studied the people of the high north for several years.

George Wilkins, photographer, left the boat with Stefansson and traveled with him for a time.

Burt McConnell, Stefansson's secretary, left the boat with Stefansson and traveled with him for about a year.

Pañurak (Jerry), an Iñupiaq hunter, left the boat with Stefansson.

Asatshak (Jimmy), an Iñupiaq hunter, left the boat with Stefansson.

Henri Beuchat, anthropologist, one of a party of four who left Shipwreck Camp on their own to go to Wrangel Island but never made it to the island.

Dr. Alistair Mackay, ship's surgeon, one of a party of four who left Shipwreck Camp on their own to go to Wrangel Island but never made it to the island.

James Murray, oceanographer, one of a party of four who left Shipwreck Camp on their own to go to Wrangel Island but never made it to the island.

George Malloch, geologist, died at Rodgers Harbor, Wrangel Is., from eating pemmican.

Bjarne Mamen, forester, died at Rodgers Harbor, Wrangel Is., from eating pemmican.

William Laird McKinlay ("Wee Mac"), meteorologist, rescued by the *King and Winge*.

Kurraluk (Harrison Kurraluk), Iñupiaq hunter, rescued by the *King and Winge*.

Qiruk (Mabel Kurraluk), sewer of furs and boots, rescued by the *King and Winge*.

Pagŋasuk (Helen Kurraluk), daughter of Kurraluk and Qiruk, about age eight, rescued by the *King and Winge*. She grew to adulthood, married, and raised a family.

Makpii (Ruth Kurraluk), also daughter of Kurraluk and Qiruk, about age two, rescued by the *King and Winge*. Makpii grew to adulthood and married Fred Ipalook, one of the first Iñupiaq teachers. Together they raised five children. The elementary school in Barrow, Alaska, is named the Fred Ipalook School.

Kataktovik, Iñupiaq hunter, friend of Kurraluk, traveled by dog and sled more than seven hundred miles with Captain Bartlett, from Wrangel Island to Siberia to Nome. From Nome he returned to Point Barrow.

Ship's Crew

Captain Robert Bartlett walked and traveled by dog sled a total of seven hundred miles to seek help for the *Karluk* survivors.

Alexander Anderson, first officer, one of the captain's party sent to set up the first camp on Wrangel Island and never seen again.

Charles Barker, second officer, one of the captain's party sent to set up the first camp on Wrangel Island and never seen again.

John Munro, chief engineer, rescued by the *King and Winge*.

Robert Williamson, second engineer, rescued by the *King and Winge*.

John Brady, able seaman, one of the captain's party sent to set up the first camp at Wrangel Island and never seen again.

A. King, able seaman, one of the captain's party sent to set up the first camp at Wrangel Island and never seen again.

Stanley Morris, able seaman, one of a party of four who left Shipwreck Camp on their own to go to Wrangel Island but never made it to the island.

Robert Templeman, steward and cook, rescued by the *King and Winge*.

Ernest Chafe, messroom boy, rescued by the *King and Winge*.

H. Williams, able seaman, rescued by the *King and Winge*.

F. W. Maurer, fireman, rescued by the *King and Winge*.

G. Breddy, fireman, found shot in his tent on Wrangel Island. Others in the tent said he shot himself.

John Hadley, whaler and ship's carpenter, rescued by the *King and Winge*.

Ship's Animals

Niġiguguaraq (NEE-gee-goo-gu-rak), "little animal," a black cat brought on board at Esquimault in British Columbia before the ship left port, rescued by the *King and Winge*, then taken onto the *Bear* by Pagṇasuk and Makpii. The cat scratched Makpii on the chin. She always had a scar from that scratch.

Of the **forty sled dogs** that started the trip, twelve went with Stefansson to hunt caribou. Seven went with Bartlett across the ice bridge to Siberia. Some ran off. Some died. Some were lost on the ice. Three survived. They and three puppies born on Wrangel Island were taken on board the *King and Winge* with the others in the *Karluk* party.

Makpii.

The Iñupiaq family: Makpii, Qiruk, Kurraluk, and in front, Paŋnasuk.

The *Karluk* survivors on board the *Bear*. Standing in back, Munro. From left to right: Templeman, Williamson, Hadley (the carpenter), Captain Bartlett, Qiruk, McKinlay (Wee Mac), Chafe, Williams, Maurer. In front: Makpii, Paŋnasuk, Kurraluk.